Have you hear
Of a bo
He thought he could reach the stars.

His name was, Mars
And in the day
He would play

With all his toys
Bicycles, tricycles, and did I mention
Those fast cars

He'd laugh and run
Each day under the Sun
Often thinking

"I wonder, how far?"

How far are those planes and birds?
How far are those clouds?

At night

How far are those stars?

I bet if I reach and stretchhh...

No. Not yet
But, soon

Soon I will be big and tall
And all obstacles
Great and small

Will be no worry for me

You see...

Every night, I go to bed
And in my head
I see myself

Reaching out to touch those planes, birds, clouds
And yes, even the stars

Then

As I open my eyes to greet the day

Undoubtedly I've grown

At least a half an inch I'd say

So, at that pace
I mean, it's no race
But, I'd be at least 40 feet tall in no time

Mars thought to himself
Surely then I'd reach those stars

Mars proceeded to play with all his toys

The bicycles, tricycles, and did I mention
Those fast cars

And eventually
All that playing wore him out

The tired boy shut his eyes

What is this?

It was so bright
Everywhere he looked there was light
Left, right, all lines of sight

Did he?
Was it true?

He looked down and couldn't find his toes
A bird flew by his nose

A plane zipped near his left hip

And he realized
That the pillows he had been laying his head
upon

Were really clouds

But why was it so bright?

Then, the smart boy remembered his mother's poem...

"Star light, star bright
First star I see tonight;
I wish I may, I wish I might
Have the wish I wish tonight."

So, Mars reached out

Made in the USA
Las Vegas, NV
08 December 2024

13656292R00017